P9-BJV-566

Feelings
ALPHABET

Feelings

ALPHABET

An Album of Emotions from A to Z

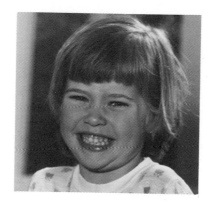

Judy Lalli, M.S.

♥♥♥ B.L. WINCH & ASSOCIATES
Rolling Hills Estates, California

Copyright © 1984 by Judith M. Lalli
All Rights Reserved

Published by B.L. Winch & Associates
45 Hitching Post Drive, Building 2
Rolling Hills Estates, California 90274

No part of this book may be reproduced by any mechanical,
photographic, or electronic process, or in the form of a
photographic recording, nor may it be stored in a retrieval
system, transmitted or otherwise copied for public or private use
without the written permission of the publisher.

Production Coordinator: Janet Lovelady
Photography: Douglas L. Mason-Fry
Graphics: Nancy Snyder

Special thanks to: Harry Brown and Linda Nyce-Landis

First U.S. Printing

Library of Congress Cataloging in Publication Data

Lalli, Judy. 1949-
    Feelings alphabet.

    Summary: Each letter of the alphabet is represented by a
captioned photograph illustrating a different feeling or emotion.
    1. Emotions—Juvenile literature. 2. Alphabet—Juvenile literature
[1. Alphabet. 2. Emotions]
I. Title.
BF561.L35 1984   372.4'145   83-51343
ISBN 0-935266-15-1 (pbk.)

For Tony

INTRODUCTION

I created FEELINGS ALPHABET out of my conviction that the children who are able to acknowledge and express their feelings will be the ones who will be able to learn. When we succeed at learning, we feel good about ourselves. At the same time, we can't learn *unless* we feel good about ourselves. Hence, FEELINGS ALPHABET is an *enabling* book.

FEELINGS ALPHABET is also an ABC book, designed to teach alphabet letters to young children. Beginning readers will learn to read and comprehend the words depicted on each page. But, more importantly, FEELINGS ALPHABET is a tool for teaching children about themselves. Familiar feelings are captured in delightful, "one-of-a-kind" photographs and their meanings are highlighted with individualized lettering. Naming each feeling fosters an awareness that emotions are universal, they are special, *and* they matter. Exploring an alphabet of feelings with a child reinforces this important lesson: feelings in themselves are not good or bad — they just are.

Children instantly identify with the kids in FEELINGS ALPHABET:

> "I like the boy who is frustrated. When I don't get my way, sometimes I cry and slam my door."

> "The silly picture shows what I like to do. I like to make my baby sister giggle."

As they recognize and share experiences of embarrassment, pride, or disappointment, younger readers will enlarge their knowledge of human nature and develop greater tolerance of others.

Children will gain a sense of accomplishment as they learn to read these feelings words and relate to the ideas. They will find joy as they become adept at expressing themselves more fully. Self-awareness and self-acceptance will grow, page by page.

1

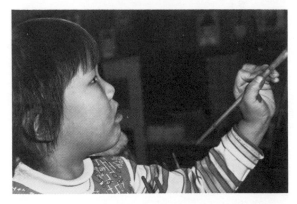

How do you feel today?

afraid

6

?
Curious

Disappointed

embarrassed

Fustatid

~~Frustated~~

~~Frastratid~~

~~Frustrited~~

Frustrated!

giggly

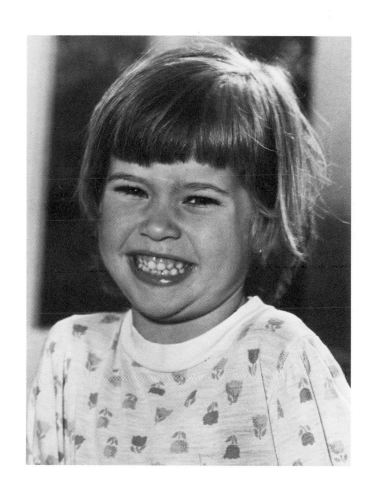

Helpful

INVOLVED

JOYFUL!

kissable

Loving

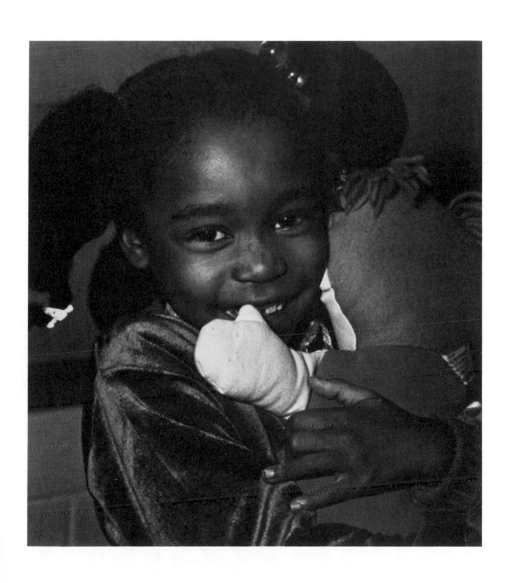

MISERABLE

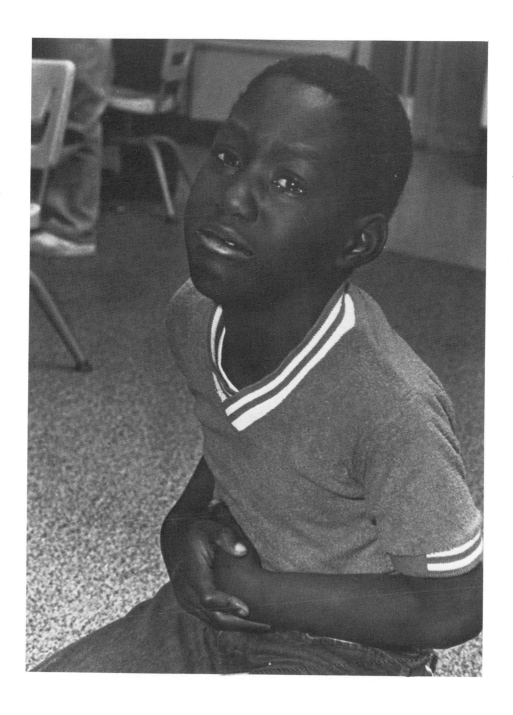

Nervous

O.K.

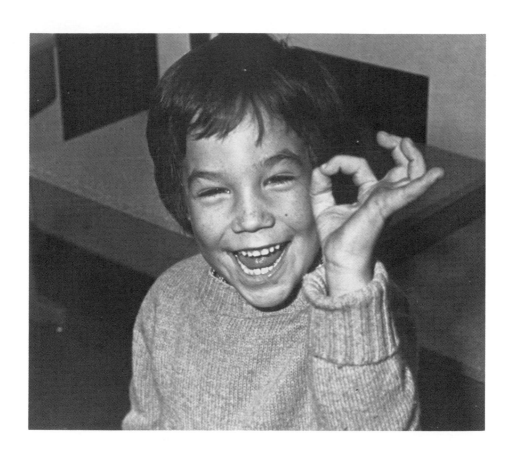

PROUD

Quiet

relaxed

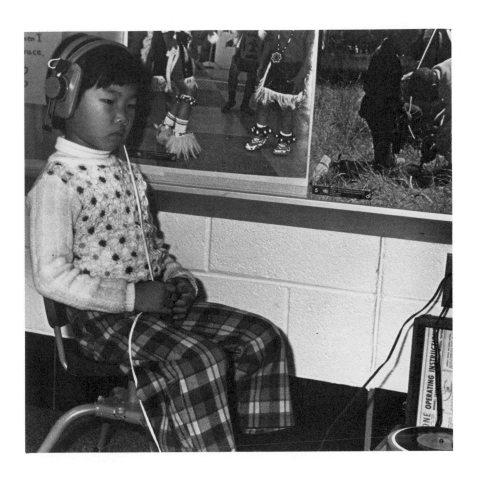

Silly

UNHAPPY

VAIN

wishy-washy

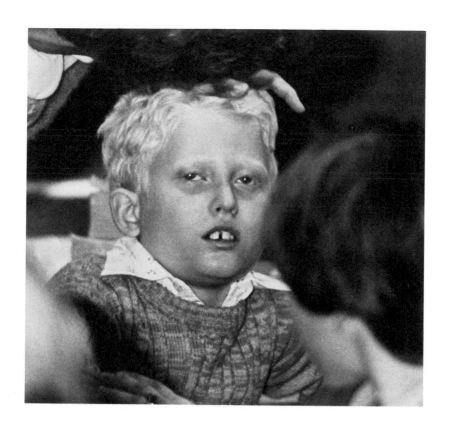

The end

ABOUT THE AUTHOR

JUDY LALLI, M.S., a first-grade teacher in Norristown, Pennsylvania, has been teaching for twelve years. She holds B.S. and M.S. degrees in elementary education from the University of Pennsylvania, and she has completed extensive postgraduate work in the fields of reading instruction and human development. Her background in these areas led her to write her first book, *At Least I'm Getting Better* (Impact, 1981), a delightful blend of poems and photographs dealing with children's feelings and relationships. *Feelings Alphabet* also grew out of her work with emotions and self-concept in children.

Judy Lalli has directed and performed in many local and dinner theater productions. She loves her family, the color purple, walking on the beach, talking on the phone, and making her friends laugh. She describes herself as "...compulsive about some things, absent-minded about others, very emotional — and always, always ready to celebrate life!"

ABOUT THE PHOTOGRAPHER

DOUGLAS L. MASON-FRY has taught industrial arts for ten years. He has been taking pictures for much longer than that. Currently, he does wedding and fine art photography in Lancaster, Pennsylvania. *Feelings Alphabet* is Doug's second collaboration with Judy Lalli: his charming and sensitive photographs appear in *At Least I'm Getting Better.*

ABOUT THE GRAPHIC ARTIST

NANCY SNYDER is an illustrator and designer living in Norristown, Pennsylvania. She holds a Bachelor of Fine Arts degree in illustration from Moore College of Art, where she currently teaches part-time. In addition to her freelance work, Nancy does courtroom art for WCAU-TV in Philadelphia.

THE CREATIVE PARENTING/CREATIVE TEACHING SERIES FROM B.L. WINCH & ASSOCIATES

The Creative Parenting/Creative Teaching Series presents an array of practical purposeful materials to help you in your job as a parent or other caring adult working with children. Parents are playing an increasingly vital role in their children's educations; teachers look for ways to effectively incorporate and assist parents' efforts at home as well as at school. Counselors, health practitioners, and educational specialists, too, look for useful materials that help them relate better to families and children.

B.L. Winch's Creative Parenting/Creative Teaching Series provides the support materials for all adult endeavors to enhance children's lives in meaningful and creative ways.

LEARNING TO LIVE, LEARNING TO LOVE
by Joanne Haynes-Klassen

An inspirational message for all ages about the importance of love in every thing we do. Beautifully told through words and pictures, **Learning to Live, Learning to Love** describes the human journey toward openness, forgiveness, and fulfillment.

$7.95 Illustrated Trade Paperback — 150 pages

UNICORNS ARE REAL:
A RIGHT-BRAINED APPROACH TO LEARNING
by Barbara Meiseter Vitale

An illustrated activity book showing parents and teachers how to tap into children's "right-brained" strengths (using color, imagery, touch, sound, and movement) to teach "left-brain" school tasks.

$9.95 Trade Paperback — 118 Pages

CHARLES THE CLOWN'S GUIDE TO CHILDREN'S PARTIES
by Charles and Linda Kraus

A resource book of helpful party guidelines plus age-appropriate activities that naturally motivate and absorb children. Helps you to learn about all children as well as plan for that special event!

$9.95   Illustrated Trade Paperback — 304 Pages

"HE HIT ME BACK FIRST!" CREATIVE VISUALIZATION ACTIVITIES FOR TEACHING & PARENTING
by Eva D. Fugitt

Based on psychosynthesis, this activity book lovingly guides children to self-correcting behavior. Children become aware of choice and their "Wise Part Within" which helps them choose appropriate behaviors in all their interactions.

$9.95   Trade Paperback — 116 Pages

PITCHING IN: HOW TO TEACH YOUR CHILDREN TO WORK AROUND THE HOUSE
by Charles Spellmann and Rachel Williams

Adults who worked around the house as children are more successful later in life, research shows. Here's a simple system plus sound parenting advice and humor, too!

$5.45   Illustrated Trade Paperback — 102 Pages

THE PARENT BOOK: THE HOLISTIC PROGRAM FOR RAISING THE EMOTIONALLY MATURE CHILD
by Harold Bessell and Thomas P. Kelly Jr.

A child-raising guide for children ages 3-14 that tells you how to live with your children in a way that encourages their healthy emtoional development.

$9.95   Illustrated Trade Paperback — 204 Pages

FIRST TIME OUT: SKILLS FOR LIVING AWAY FROM HOME
by Reva Camiel and Hila Michaelsen

A positive, comprehensive guide for young adults leaving home for the first time. Helps turn a hazardous time for parents and teens into a constructive and satisfying adventure for all.

$5.95   Trade Paperback — 220 Pages

PAJAMAS DON'T MATTER
(OR: WHAT YOUR BABY REALLY NEEDS)
by Trish Gribben

Valuable information and needed reassurances to new parents as they struggle through the frantic, but rewarding, first years of their child's life.

$5.95   Illustrated Trade Paperback — 52 Pages

FEELINGS ALPHABET
by Judy Lalli

Ever feel "ticklish," "wishy-washy" or "zonked"? These are a few of the feelings shown so effectively in this unique alphabet book which combines real-life photos with fascinating word graphics to convey the emotions of young children. By listening to and talking about the book, children will learn to express and accept their feelings.

$5.95   Black/White Photos — 72 Pages

WHOSE CHILD CRIES
Children of Gay Parents Talk About Their Lives
by Joe Gantz

This sensitive study presents the experiences of children in five families as they come to terms with their parent's life-styles. Their straightforward and heartfelt explanations of what it is like growing up in their homes help make this book a valuable resource and excellent counseling tool. Foreword by Eda LeShan columnist for *Women's Day Magazine*.

$16.95 Hardbound $8.95 Softcover — 260 Pages

Write to B.L. Winch & Associates for free catalog describing these and other parenting/teaching materials for the handicapped and the gifted, as well as our full line of TA and Warm Fuzzy products for all ages.

B.L. WINCH & ASSOCIATES
45 Hitching Post Drive Building 2
Rolling HIlls Estates, California 90274